PIRATES™

www.mascotbooks.com

©2013 Mascot Books. All Rights Reserved. No part of this
publication may be reproduced, stored in a retrieval system
or transmitted in any form by any means electronic, mechanical,
or photocopying, recording or otherwise without the permission
of Mascot Books.

For more information, please contact:
Mascot Books
560 Herndon Parkway #120
Herndon, VA 20170
info@mascotbooks.com

CPSIA Code: PRT0514B
ISBN-10: 1620864827
ISBN-13: 9781620864821

Major League Baseball trademarks and copyrights are used with
permission of Major League Baseball Properties, Inc.

Printed in the United States

Hello,
Pirate Parrot!™

Naren Aryal
Illustrated by **Danny Moore**

It was a beautiful day in Pittsburgh, Pennsylvania.
Pirate Parrot was on his way to the ballpark for a baseball game.

As he walked through the city, *Pirates* fans cheered, "Hello, *Pirate Parrot*!"

The mascot was so excited to be going to the game, and couldn't wait to watch his favorite team play.

In front of the ballpark, he ran into lots of *Pirates* fans. They cheered, "Hello, *Pirate Parrot*!"

Pirate Parrot arrived on the field just in time for batting practice.
Each player took swings to get ready for the game.

As the team's best hitter stepped to home plate,
he said, "Hello, *Pirate Parrot!*"

After batting practice, the grounds crew
proudly prepared the field for play.

As the grounds crew worked, they hollered,
"Hello, *Pirate Parrot!*"

Pirate Parrot was feeling hungry. He grabbed a few snacks and a *Pirates* pennant at the concession stand.

As he made his way back to the field,
a family shouted, "Hello, *Pirate Parrot*!"

Each *Pirates* player stood on the first-base line
as the home team was introduced.

Pirate Parrot received the largest applause!
Fans roared, "Hello, *Pirate Parrot*!"

"PLAY BALL!" yelled the umpire. The *Pirates* pitcher delivered a fastball to start the game. "STRIKE ONE!" called the umpire.

The umpire noticed the mascot nearby and said,
"Hello, *Pirate Parrot*!"

Pirate Parrot went into the bleachers to visit his fans.
Everyone was excited to see him.

A family waved and called out, "Hello, *Pirate Parrot*!"

It was now time for the seventh-inning stretch. The mascot led the crowd as everyone sang "Take Me Out To The Ballgame™!"

Young *Pirates* fans danced on the dugout with *Pirate Parrot*.
They cheered, "Let's go, *Pirates*!"

In the bottom of the ninth inning, a *Pirates* player hit a game-winning home run over the right-field fence.

The team gathered at home plate to celebrate the victory.
The players chanted, "*Pirates* win, *Pirates* win!"

After the game, *Pirate Parrot* was tired. It had been a long day at the ballpark. He walked home and went straight to bed.

Goodnight, *Pirate Parrot*!

Have a book idea?

Contact us at:

Mascot Books
560 Herndon Parkway #120
Herndon, VA 20170

info@mascotbooks.com | www.mascotbooks.com

PIRATES™